THIS BOOK BELONGS TO

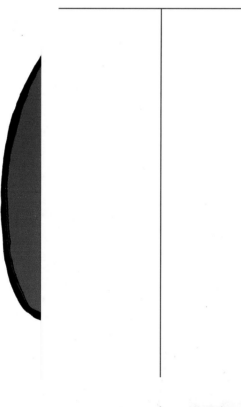

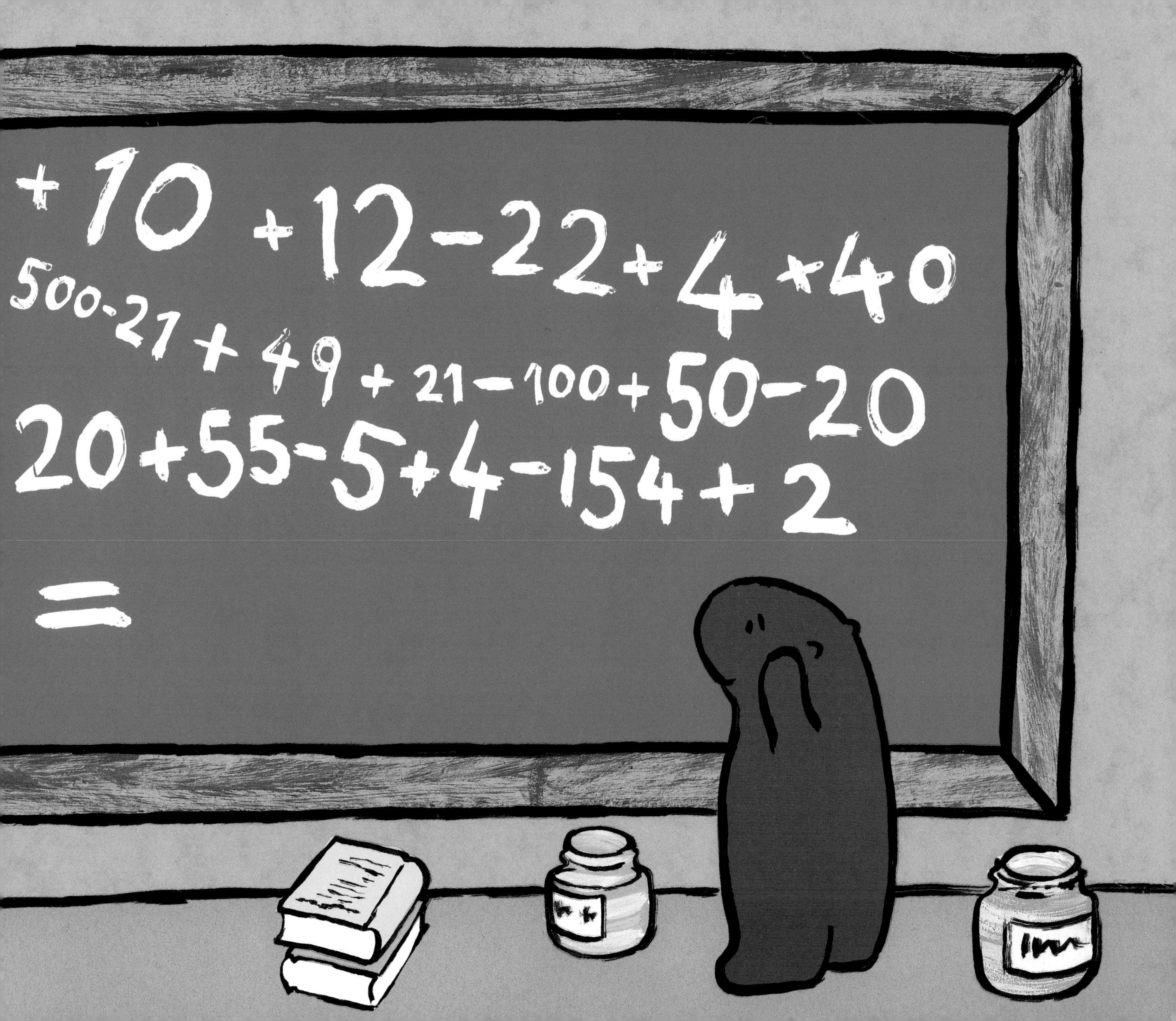
+10 +12-22+4+40
500-27+49+21-100+50-20
20+55-5+4-154+2
=

For Sarah, who
introduced me
to Eric

ERIC THE RED
A Red Fox Book: 0 09 943923 9

First published in Great Britain by The Bodley Head,
an imprint of Random House Children's Books
The Bodley Head edition published 2003
Red Fox edition published 2004

1 3 5 7 9 10 8 6 4 2

Copyright © Caroline Glicksman, 2003

Red Fox Books are published
by Random House Children's Books,
61–63 Uxbridge Road, London W5 5SA,
a division of The Random House Group Ltd,
in Australia by Random House Australia (Pty) Ltd,
20 Alfred Street, Milsons Point,
Sydney, NSW 2061, Australia,
in New Zealand by Random House
New Zealand Ltd, 18 Poland Road, Glenfield,
Auckland 10, New Zealand, and in
South Africa by Random House
(Pty) Ltd, Endulini, 5A Jubilee Road,
Parktown 2193, South Africa

THE RANDOM HOUSE GROUP
Limited Reg. No. 954009
www.**kidsatrandomhouse**.co.uk

A CIP catalogue record for this
book is available from the
British Library.

Printed and bound
in Malaysia

Eric the Red

Caroline Glicksman

RED FOX

Eric is a very unusual bear.

Most bears are brown or black or white.

For one thing, Eric is red.

Very red.

So red that he glows
in the dark.

And Eric is very, very clever, especially with numbers.

He even dreams about numbers!

Eric likes counting things on his way to work. This morning he saw:

two yellow lorries

four bears fishing

six red cars

eight boats on the river

Eric has a very important job at the Big Bear Bank.

Every day, he counts up all the bank's money and puts it in the big safe.

Then he thinks up a new set of numbers for the lock and closes the safe tight.

Eric is the only bear who knows the numbers!

Every so often, Eric helps at the front counter of the bank. He doesn't like working there because sometimes badly behaved bears laugh at his red fur.

Then Eric wishes he was at home, eating lots of honey, and doing bigger and bigger sums on his computer.

But today the first customer
had such kind, friendly eyes
that Eric didn't mind.

"My name is Erica,"
she said. "I'd
like to start
saving . . ."

SPEAK HERE

MORE MATHS

5

POLAR ICES

POLAR ICES

POLAR ICES

QUEUE THIS WAY

SECURI

BAMBOO CHOOS

VROOM!

Just then an ice-cream van burst through the door of the bank and two polar bears jumped out. Erica gasped.

"EVERYONE FREEZE!" shouted the first polar bear.

He gave Eric a note.

It said:

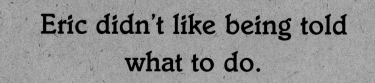

Eric didn't like being told
what to do.

Without thinking, he growled at the first polar bear.

The polar bear was so surprised that he stepped back, slipped on an ice lolly, and banged his head on the floor.

In a flash, the second polar bear grabbed Erica, jumped over the glass screen, and spun Eric round on his chair. Fast.

"TELL ME THE NUMBERS TO OPEN THE SAFE, TOMATO FACE!" he shouted.

"OR I'LL HAVE THIS LITTLE BEAR FOR ELEVENSES!"

Eric's head spun. Millions of numbers whirled round in his head. How would he remember the ones he needed to save Erica?

"YOU'VE GOT FIVE
SECONDS!" shouted
the polar bear.
"FIVE!
FOUR!!
THREE!!!
TWO!!!!"

MORE MATHS

"Wait!" gasped Eric.
"That's it! TWO!
The two times table! The numbers
I saw this morning. Two . . . four . . ."

The polar bear dropped Erica
and started turning
the lock on the safe.

"Six . . . eight . . . ten . . ."
continued Eric, but
his head was spinning
so much that
he couldn't remember
the last number.

"**TWELVE . . .**" said Erica. Suddenly, the safe opened and the polar bear started grabbing the money as fast as he could. Soon he was right inside the safe.

Eric's head stopped spinning.

LOOT

He helped Erica to her feet and . . .

Wah! Wah! Wah!

Five police bears rushed in and arrested the first polar bear, who was still lying dazed on the floor.

"You caught them red-handed!" said Erica. She gave Eric's paw a gentle squeeze.

"I couldn't have done it alone," said Eric. Suddenly, he noticed . . .

. . . the maths book that Erica
was holding in her paws.
"You like maths too!" he said.
"I've never met another bear
who liked numbers," said Erica.

Eric glowed very red.

"Wouldn't it be fun to do sums
together?" said Erica.
Eric grinned. "Yes, twice as
much fun!" he said.

$$1 + 1 + 2 + 4 + 6 + 8$$
$$+ 34 + 100 - 20 + 5 + 16 + 4 + 16 +$$
$$+ 5 - 55 + 2 + 48 - 520 +$$
$$- 42 + 2 - 60$$

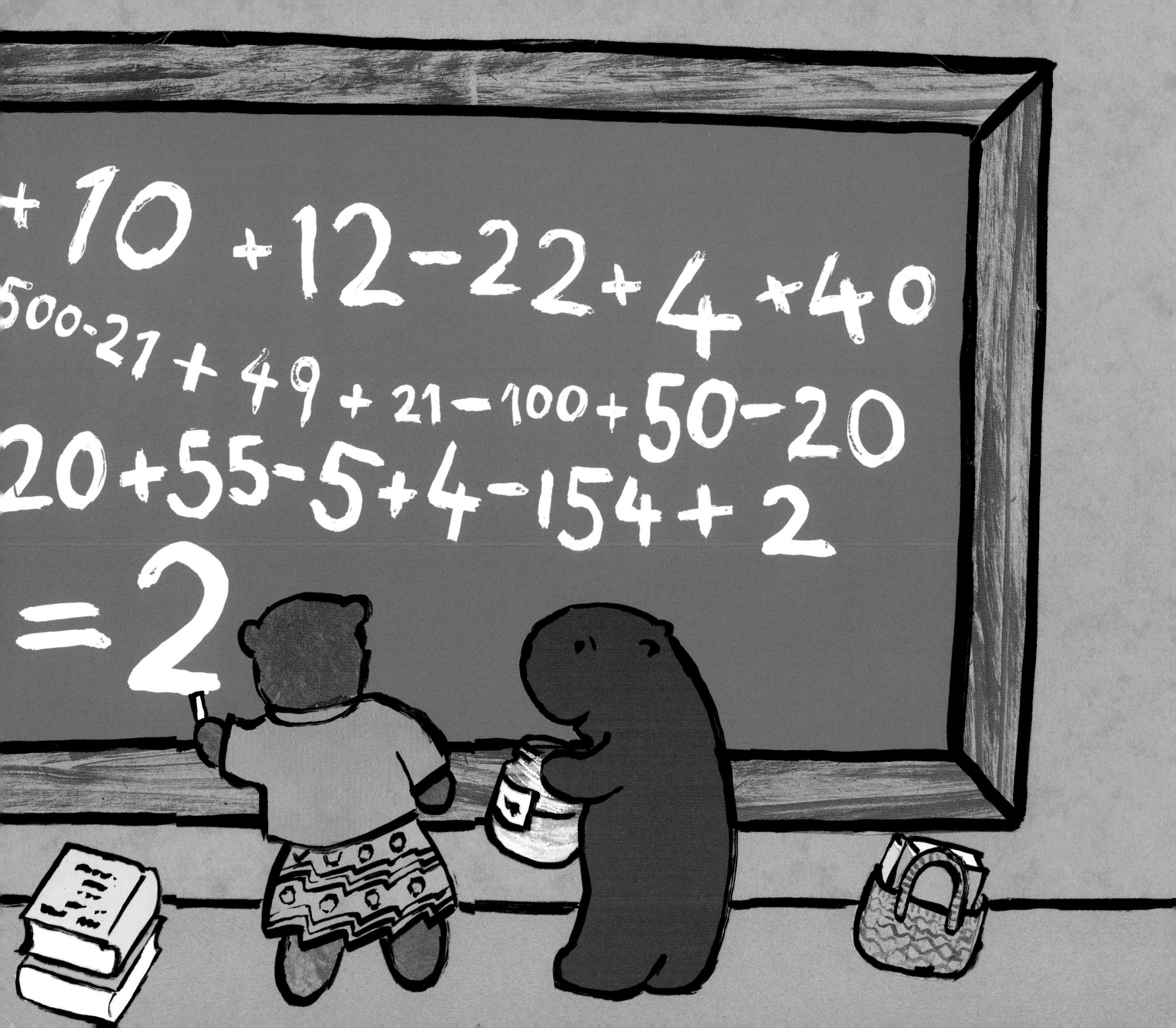
+10 +12−22+4+40
500-27+49+21−100+50−20
20+55−5+4−154+2
=2

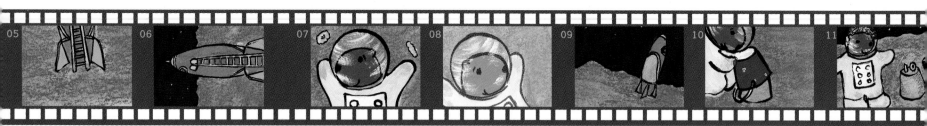

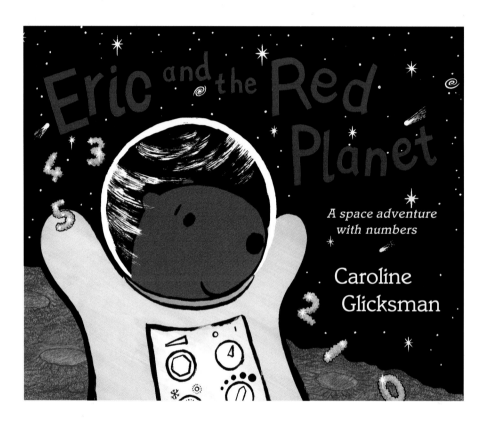

JOIN ERIC ON HIS NEXT ADVENTURE!

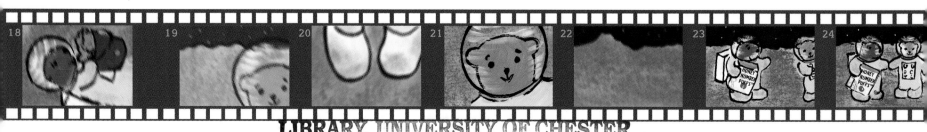

All Random House Children's Book titles are available by post from: Book Service, PO Box 29, Douglas, Isle of Man, IM99 1BQ Credit cards accepted. Tel +44 (01)624 836000, fax +44 (01)01624 837003 or www.bookpost.co.uk or email bookshop@enterprise.net for details Free postage and packing in the UK. Overseas customers: allow £1 per book (paperbacks) and £3 per book (hardbacks)